# DR JEKYLL AND MR HYDE

## ROBERT LOUIS STEVENSON

www.realreads.co.uk

Retold by Peter Crowther
Illustrated by Vanessa Lubach

Printed in Malaysia for Imago Ltd
Designed by Lucy Guenot
Typeset by Bookcraft Ltd, Stroud, Gloucestershire

# CONTENTS

The Characters       4

Dr Jekyll and Mr Hyde     7

Taking things further     55

# THE CHARACTERS

## Dr Henry Jekyll

Can this respectable doctor resist the strange powers of Mr Hyde?

## Edward Hyde

Who is this man and what is the mysterious hold he has over Dr Jekyll?

## Mr Utterson

Mr Utterson is Dr Jekyll's friend and lawyer. Can he solve the mystery? Can he save his friend?

## Richard Enfield

What information does Richard Enfield possess? Will he save or condemn Dr Jekyll?

## Poole

Poole is Dr Jekyll's faithful butler. Can he save his master from himself?

## Dr Hastie Lanyon

Dr Lanyon witnesses a terrifyingly strange event. How will he react?

## Inspector Newcomen

Inspector Newcomen is one of Scotland Yard's finest. Can he discover Edward Hyde's true identity, and solve a brutal murder?

# DR JEKYLL AND MR HYDE

'You know,' Enfield said to his friend Utterson the lawyer as they strolled through a down-at-heel part of London, 'that house over there is etched in my mind in connection with a strange story.'

'Indeed?' Utterson remarked, looking at the sinister block of buildings at which his friend was pointing. 'Do tell.'

'I was coming home late, about three o'clock of a black winter morning, and my way lay through this part of town. Just here, where we are standing, I saw the oddest thing. Some fellow trampled calmly all over a young girl, then left her screaming on the ground.'

'Whatever for?'

Enfield shook his head. 'No reason, save that she ran into him by accident.'

'So the girl's fault, then?'

'Perhaps. But the man – a singularly distasteful fellow to be sure – made to walk off, until I collared him and then called a doctor to the scene to attend the child.'

'Was the fellow drunk?'

'Not to my knowledge. A crowd built up baying for his blood, but the doctor and I held them off.'

'And this house,' Utterson said, 'how is it relevant?'

'Under threat of a lawsuit on the part of the girl's parents – which would surely have been successful – we managed to persuade him to pay one hundred pounds as compensation for his behaviour. At first the fellow was reluctant, but I think he feared the crowd, and finally he led us to this very dwelling, disappeared inside, and returned with ten pounds in coin and a cheque for the balance.'

'Hmph!' Utterson snorted. 'I'll wager the cheque was—'

'No,' Enfield interrupted. 'I was wary myself, but we all repaired to my rooms until the bank opened later that day. When we went down to the bank they confirmed that the cheque was genuine, and the family got their ninety pounds.'

'And that was the end of it?'

Enfield shrugged and nodded, and the pair started to walk again.

'What was the fellow's name?'

'Hyde,' Enfield replied, his voice little more than a whisper. 'Edward Hyde. But that wasn't the name on the cheque.'

Utterson stopped again. 'Edward Hyde, you say?'

Enfield nodded. 'Whatever is the matter, my dear Utterson?'

'Nothing, my dear chap. I thought for a moment I knew the fellow – or knew of him.'

As they passed by a jetty where a young boy sat, his line cast out into the murky water, Enfield said, 'You didn't ask me the name on the bounder's cheque.'

Utterson nodded, smiling grimly, and, after a few seconds, he said, 'That is because I believe I know it already.' What he did not say was that he knew the owner of the house whose rear entrance was the very door that Enfield had pointed out.

Back at his own house, Utterson lost no time in retrieving some documents from his safe. He leafed through them until he found an envelope bearing the words 'Dr Henry Jekyll's Will'. He opened the envelope and, by the flickering light of a candle, he discovered the sentence he sought: in the event of Jekyll's death, all possessions were to pass into the hands of the doctor's 'friend and benefactor' Edward Hyde. Moreover, the document continued, if the doctor were to disappear for a time exceeding three months, Hyde should step fully into Henry Jekyll's shoes. He would be free of any financial obligations save the payment of a few small sums to the doctor's household.

'I have no idea what might be going on, nor what hold this Hyde fellow might have on you, Henry Jekyll,' Utterson whispered to the room, 'but I swear I will make it my business to find out.'

For the next few days, Utterson did make it his business to spend as much time as possible in the vicinity of the building his friend Enfield had pointed out. If he be Mr Hyde, he thought, I shall be Mr Seek.

One evening, at a little after ten o'clock, his patience was finally rewarded. He heard footsteps echoing down the street. Utterson withdrew into a shop doorway and waited. A man appeared out of the gloom into the small pool of gaslight, reached into his pocket, and produced a key. He was small – almost stunted – and plainly dressed, his face shrouded by the brim of his hat. Although he glanced furtively from side to side, he failed to spot Utterson until he was across the street and almost at the door to the house.

'Mr Hyde, I think?' Utterson said softly as he stepped out of the shadows.

The man shrank back with a sharp intake of breath, still managing to keep his face hidden. 'What do you want?' he asked, his voice harsh.

Utterson nodded to the door of the house. 'I'm a friend of Dr Jekyll. I thought we might talk inside.'

'Who are you?'

'Utterson of Gaunt Street,' said Utterson. 'You must surely have heard my name.' As Hyde shook his head, Utterson continued. 'I thought you might admit me.'

'You will not find Dr Jekyll here; he is away from home. How do you know me?'

Utterson did not answer that question, instead asking another. 'Will you do me a favour?'

'What is it?' asked Hyde suspiciously.

'Will you let me see your face?' asked the lawyer.

Edward Hyde hesitated, and then, as if suddenly changing his mind, looked straight at Utterson with an air of defiance. In the lamplight

Utterson noticed how Hyde's brows met in thick black hair and his face was pale, the eyes glinting like those of a fish – barely human, in fact.

'Now I shall recognise you again,' said Utterson. 'It may be useful.'

'Yes,' returned Hyde, 'perhaps it is as well we have met. I think you should also have my address,' and he gave the lawyer a number of a street in Soho. Good god, thought Utterson, is he thinking that I shall need his address in order to fulfil the terms of Dr Jekyll's will?

'Now you shall tell me how you know me,' said Hyde.

'We have friends in common,' Utterson said. 'Dr Jekyll, for a start.'

Hyde's eyes flashed wide. 'What has Jekyll told you about me?' he cried, with a flush of anger. Without waiting for an answer, Hyde unlocked the door and disappeared into the house.

What on earth could possibly link Jekyll
with such an unpleasant man, Utterson
wondered. One thing was certain – whatever
it was, such a link could only be bad for the
doctor. He decided that there was only one
course left open to him. He must talk to
Henry Jekyll.

Round the corner from the sinister building
where Hyde had disappeared there was a
square of ancient, handsome houses, going
somewhat to seed. One house still wore a
great air of wealth and comfort, though it was
now in darkness except for the fan-light. At
the door of this house Mr Utterson stopped
and knocked.

Presently, Jekyll's elderly butler – slightly
stooped but with sharp clear eyes – pulled
open the door. His face immediately broke into
a broad smile.

'Oh, Mr Utterson, sir,' the man said cheerfully. 'I fear the master is away from home.'

Utterson nodded regretfully. 'No matter, Poole. I shall see him another time.' Then he said, 'I believe I saw Mr Hyde come in by the old dissecting room door earlier. Is that right, with the doctor away?'

'Quite right, sir. The gentleman has a key.'

'Your master seems to have placed a great deal of trust in this fellow,' he observed as he moved back onto the step.

'Yes sir,' Poole agreed. 'We all of us have orders to obey him, though he never dines here. In fact, we see very little of him on this side of the house. He mostly comes and goes through the laboratory.'

On the way home through the fog, Utterson's mind whirled. He was glad when he reached the familiarity of his own front door and went inside.

'I have been wanting to speak with you, Henry,' Utterson said. He had stayed behind for a final drink after one of Dr Jekyll's famous dinner parties.

'With regard to what, my dear friend?'

'Your will,' came the reply.

Jekyll snorted. 'My will?'

'Yes. It's Hyde. I have been hearing something of the fellow.'

Jekyll got to his feet. 'I do not care to hear more.'

'But what I heard was—'

Jekyll waved a hand. 'No. You do not understand my position. I am somewhat ... somewhat painfully situated. In brief, my position in this matter is very strange. I know you have seen him,' Jekyll continued. 'He told me so. And I fear he was rude to you. Nevertheless, I want you to promise that, in the event that I am taken away, you will look after him and his rights.'

Utterson saw the folly of arguing: his friend's mind was made up. 'I can't pretend that I shall ever like him,' he said softly.

'I do not ask for that. I ask only for justice.'

'Very well,' Utterson said at last. 'I promise.'

Jekyll watched his friend disappear up the street before checking that the outer door was locked. Then he told Poole that he did not want to be disturbed and retired into his laboratory.

There, amidst bubbling pipettes and flasks, the doctor pulled from the shelves a small array of vials, the liquids from which he began to mix together carefully in a glass. When he was satisfied with the result, he lifted the

glass to his mouth and, with a momentary pause, tilted it back and swallowed the whole mixture.

Almost immediately he slumped against the heavy wooden counter, his face a mask of pain. Eyes tightly shut and mouth clenched, he clutched his stomach and folded over, stifling a deep moan. Even as he bent forward, his body was already thickening, changing – sinew, muscle, artery, all of them expanding or contracting. Churning noises rumbled from his stomach, cartilage and bone twanged and cracked as his neck grew shorter and his neatly-styled hair exploded into a dense thatch.

In those brief seconds while the change was under way, Henry Jekyll was flooded with regret. But then, when the change was complete, there were no such reservations. It was like an easing of pain, his long-held everyday identity, with all of its restrictions, fell away from him and left in its place a profound alertness unfettered by the constraints and sensibilities imposed by society. He felt a smile take his mouth and spread it wide.

Henry Jekyll, respected doctor and gentleman of the parish, was now Edward Hyde. The world and all its untamed pleasures belonged to him.

He changed his clothes for some more suited to his radically altered shape and, making sure he did not wake Poole, he slipped out into the night.

Utterson had made a very emphatic promise to his friend, and saw no reason to continue his pursuit of Edward Hyde. Over the following months he threw his energy into his work.

Utterson saw Jekyll from time to time, though perhaps not as often as they had both once enjoyed. Jekyll explained that he was very busy with his work, and the time-consuming research about which he would never speak.

What Jekyll did not tell Utterson, however, was that he was able to continue taking the miraculous potion without any serious consequences, thus living a double life.

But what had started as a brave scientific experiment soon became a lunatic addiction. As his metabolism grew accustomed to the effects of the mixture, and his temperament became more comfortable as Mr Hyde, Dr Jekyll had to increase the dosage of the antidote each time he wanted to return to his more responsible self. However, he could not have foreseen the dreadful event that would change everything.

About a year after Utterson had spoken to Dr Jekyll about his friend Hyde, London was startled by a crime of singular ferocity. The details were few and startling. A maidservant, living alone in a house not far from the river, had gone upstairs to bed about eleven. When she glanced out of the window she saw a scruffy and heavy-set man encounter a well-dressed gentleman taking an evening stroll.

She immediately recognised the scruffy man as Edward Hyde who had, on occasion, visited her master. She saw the smarter gentleman raise his

hat. Although she could not hear what was said, she assumed that it was polite conversation. She was therefore astonished to see Hyde suddenly enraged. Sweeping his walking-stick like a sabre, he attacked the other man, showing not an ounce of mercy.

Knocking the unfortunate fellow to the ground, Hyde jumped up and down on the man's chest. Finally, sitting astride him, he beat his head to a pulp.

The maid, having seen the whole thing, was able to give the police both a description of the attacker and his name. At the scene of the crime, a constable found part of a walking stick, still bloodied. In one of the unidentifiable victim's pockets was a stamped envelope with Utterson's name on it. When the police visited Utterson, the lawyer asked to see the body.

'It is as I feared,' Utterson said, his words heavy with regret. 'It is my very good friend Sir Danvers Carew.' He nodded to the morgue attendant, who covered the body. 'If you come with me in my cab,' he said to the senior policeman, 'I can take you to the murderer's house.' And he led the way to a certain address in Soho.

A dishevelled old woman answered the door.
'Oh,' she said with a hoarse and throaty chuckle.
''E's not 'ere.' She seemed reluctant to let
the men into the house, but when Inspector
Newcomen of Scotland Yard stepped forward she
relented. In fact, she seemed quietly delighted at
the possibility that her master had fallen foul of
the law.

Hyde's rooms were a mess, with clothes
lying in heaps and pockets turned inside out as
though a burglary had
taken place.

But amidst the chaos they found the other half of the walking stick and, in the fireplace, a partly burned chequebook. A visit to Hyde's bank showed there to be several thousand pounds in the man's account.

That afternoon Utterson paid a visit to the home of Henry Jekyll, and expressed the hope that the doctor was not harbouring the murderer.

'I most certainly am not,' Jekyll told his friend. Then, with seeming embarrassment he added, 'And I can assure you that the man will not be heard from again.'

To support this intention, Jekyll produced a letter he had received that very day. The letter, from Hyde, was written in an almost childlike and barely intelligible scrawl. In a few brief lines, the missive's author thanked Jekyll for his support, and explained that he had the means to escape the city. Jekyll would not hear from him again.

Utterson was relieved by all of this, but nevertheless enquired as to the envelope in which Hyde's letter had arrived. Jekyll became quite defensive. 'Why, I burned it,' he exclaimed, 'but it would have offered no clue as to the fellow's whereabouts.'

'The envelope would surely have had a postal mark?' The doctor shook his head emphatically. 'It was delivered by hand.'

'I wonder, might I borrow this?'

'His letter? Of course, by all means – take the blessed thing away.'

'And now one word more: it was Hyde who dictated the terms in your will about that disappearance?' Utterson asked. The doctor seemed seized with a qualm of faintness: he shut his mouth tight and nodded.

'I knew it,' said Utterson. 'He meant to murder you. You have had a fine escape.'

'I have had what is far more to the purpose,' returned the doctor solemnly: 'I have had a lesson,

Utterson. What a lesson I have had!' He covered his face for a moment with his hands.

As Utterson donned his coat and hat, Jekyll became more cheerful.

'On a happier note, I would like to know if you can dine with me later in the month.'

Utterson was pleased to accept, and the doctor promised to send a formal invitation to remind his friend of the arrangement and the date.

On the way out, Utterson asked Poole what the messenger was like who had delivered Hyde's envelope.

'Messenger, Mr Utterson? There has been no messenger here today.'

'Are you sure, Poole?'

'Quite sure, sir.'

Back in his offices, Utterson recounted the afternoon's events to his chief clerk, Mr Guest, who suggested that Hyde must be mad. Utterson showed Guest Hyde's letter.

'No, perhaps not mad; but it is certainly exceedingly odd handwriting.'

At that very moment, Utterson's manservant brought a note to his master. It was Dr Jekyll's invitation to dinner and, catching sight of it, Guest asked to see it. The manservant handed the note across and Guest placed it on the desk alongside Hyde's letter. His face a mask of incredulity, he turned to Utterson. Guest shuffled the two letters around for Utterson to see. 'It is clear to me, Mr Utterson, that, despite some obvious and marked differences between the two hands, there are distinct similarities.'

'Similarities?' Utterson leaned forward and glanced first at the familiar copperplate script of his friend Henry Jekyll, and then at

the uneven childlike – or perhaps even drunken – scrawl of Edward Hyde. 'I fear I simply do not see any resemblance between the two hands.'

Guest overlapped the two notes and pointed out certain elements – the curlicued script ending of words finishing in the letters 'ing', the very specific placing of the dot above the letter 'i' in both instances, the somewhat flamboyant bar on capital versions of the letters 'A' and 'H'.

'My goodness,' was all that Utterson could bring himself to say. Did this mean that his friend had forged a note for a murderer? He placed the letter purporting to be from Edward Hyde in his safe, and retired to his rooms for the evening.

A reward was immediately offered for information leading to Hyde's arrest, but no such information was forthcoming.

The days turned into weeks and the weeks into months. During this time, Dr Jekyll regained much of his previous heartiness and health, renewing his acquaintance with friends upon whom he had turned his back.

Behind the facade, however, the temptation to become Hyde again, to live beyond the restraints of civil society, whispered in his head. Whenever he looked into a mirror he seemed to see the gnarled countenance of Edward Hyde leering at him, prodding him onwards to concoct a new batch of the wicked serum.

At last the doctor succumbed – and it was a different man entirely from the staid Dr Jekyll who crept out of the house into London's mist-filled, cobbled alleyways.

Some time later, on this fateful evening,
Edward Hyde spotted a man travelling home
from a hostelry. He waited for the man behind
a wall and then leapt out into his path.

'Good evening,' Hyde said.

As the man frowned, Hyde brought his
cane across the fellow's head, hitting him
a further three times even as the man was
slumping to the ground in a bloody heap.

Without so much as a second's consideration,
Hyde removed the man's wallet and, with a
final two-handed swing of the cane into the
lifeless man's face, hurried off into the night.

Safe once more in Jekyll's laboratory, Hyde
prepared some more potion and drank it
down, collapsing to the floor amidst broken
glass. When he came to, he
was the doctor once again.
'Oh god,' he sobbed, his
hands clasped together
as if in prayer, 'help me
to stop this thing that is
happening to me.'

For a few days, Jekyll was able to control the urge to mix more of the potion. Though it was hard, his life slowly regained some of its former normality and he stayed around the house, splitting his time between his surgeries, his meals alone and his beloved books.

Then, one night, he dreamed a strange dream. In the dream, his skin crawled as though beset by the maggots he used in his surgery to clean post-operative wounds. He could feel them moving around on his arms and legs, on his neck and his face, but somehow it felt as though they were actually inside him. He sat up with a start, his eyes wide open, and he glanced nervously around the moonlit room. What had awakened him so abruptly?

As soon as the thought had formed, a fierce abdominal pain caused him to bend over. Only a grim determination prevented him from crying out, for he did not want to bring Poole rushing to his bedroom.

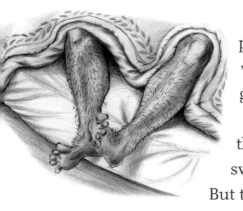

'Oh, my god, please no,' he whispered through gritted teeth.

He threw back the bedclothes and swung his legs out. But they were not his legs, not his legs at all. They were the short and strangely malformed legs of Edward Hyde. 'No!' he said again. 'This must still be a dream.'

'No, it's not a dream, my dear doctor,' a guttural voice whispered in his head. 'It's me. I'm coming again. You cannot keep me away.'

He staggered from his bed and, pulling the curtains back from the window, he saw, instead of his own reflection in the moonlight, the face of Edward Hyde glaring back at him from the glass, smiling at him. And, god help him, a part of him wanted to smile back. He knew now that he must do all he could to keep that part of himself under control.

From this time on, Jekyll's metabolism surged in waves of discomfort, the days frequently interrupted by terrible struggles to subdue Mr Hyde. The doctor continued to administer the restorative drug to himself, gradually increasing the quantity in order to hold the monster he had created at bay. Then, one sunny afternoon as he sat on a bench overlooking the lake in Regent's Park, he was overcome with nausea and uncontrollable shuddering. When he looked down, he saw that his trousers were in folds around his shoes and his hands were hairy and gnarled upon his knees.

In a panic, Hyde – now retaining many of the sensibilities of his alter ego – pulled his hat down further to cover his misshapen face and shrugged his coat collar higher before making for home as fast as he could. But he realised that he could not make the trip without being seen.

Perhaps his friend Dr Lanyon might help. Or possibly even Utterson, though he feared there might be little sympathy from that direction. It would have to be Lanyon: the brutal truth was that he had little or no choice.

Looking around, he spotted a hostelry where, he was sure, neither the hosts nor the customers would be bothered by his unruly appearance and his ill-fitting clothes. He stumped across the street and, within a few minutes, he had arranged for a private room and requested writing materials.

He promptly set about writing notes to
both Lanyon and Dr Jekyll's butler, Poole – he
no longer considered himself as the doctor,
at least not when Hyde had overtaken him.
Affecting the guise of someone suffering

from a head-cold, his collar pulled high and his scarf wrapped tightly about his lower face, he passed the notes to the innkeeper and returned to his room to wait for nightfall. As soon as darkness had filled the sky and the only lights were those cast by the meagre streetlamps now being lit, he left the inn and hailed a cab, requesting that the driver simply drive him around the darkened streets of London.

Elsewhere in the city, Dr Lanyon arrived at Jekyll's house, somewhat puzzled by the note he had received. Poole was similarly at a loss to understand what was happening, but he admitted Lanyon and led him to Dr Jekyll's laboratory.

'He asks that I take this drawer to him,' Lanyon said, his voice unsure. 'Whatever can he be wanting it for, I wonder?'

The two men paused and looked into the drawer, which was a neat arrangement of stoppered test-tubes, phials, circular tins with curious scribbles on their lids and banded confusions of rubber hose. And a book.

'I am sure I have no idea, Dr Lanyon,' Poole remarked.

Without further conversation, Lanyon took the drawer and left Jekyll's house, bound for home.

Once home, Lanyon looked more closely at the contents of the drawer. The powders were neatly enough made up, but not with the nicety of the dispensing chemist, so that it was plain they were of Jekyll's private manufacture. The book contained little but a series of dates. These covered a period of many years, but the entries had ceased about a year ago, and quite abruptly.

A knock interrupted Lanyon's investigations. When he answered the door, he found a man who was clearly in something of a distressed state. The man's clothes were enormously too large for him in every measurement, the trousers hanging on his legs and rolled up to keep them from the ground, and the coat collar sprawling wide upon his shoulders.

Dr Lanyon was further struck by the haunted expression of his face, and by his apparent state of illness.

'Edward Hyde, sir,' Hyde announced gruffly.
'I am the messenger from Dr Jekyll.'

Lanyon was unsure what to do next, but Hyde pushed his way into the house. As soon as the door was closed behind him, he grabbed hold of Lanyon's shoulders and shook him roughly.

'Do you have it?' he asked. 'Do you have it?'

Managing to disengage himself from the unpleasant man, Lanyon frowned icily. 'You forget, sir,' he said, 'that I have not had the pleasure of your acquaintance.'

'I do beg your pardon, doctor,' Hyde said, regaining some of his composure. 'I understood that a drawer—' He stopped when he saw the object in question on Lanyon's bureau.

Hyde visibly faltered, his hands clutching his chest as he requested a glass.

'Are you not well?' Lanyon asked.

'A glass!' Hyde barked.

When Lanyon returned with the glass, Hyde mixed a fizzing potion from the ingredients before him. As he raised the glass to his mouth, Hyde turned to Lanyon and said, 'You must remember the vows you made when joining our profession, my dear Lanyon.'

Lanyon was aghast at the man's familiarity.

'What follows,' Hyde continued, oblivious to the other man's sensibilities, 'is to be our secret.' And he drained the glass before staggering forward to support himself on the bureau.

Almost immediately, the transformation began.

The thuggish Edward Hyde was slowly but surely changing into the more refined form of Henry Jekyll.

'What in god's name, man—?' Lanyon began.

'God has no part in tonight's events,' Hyde croaked, though his voice was becoming softer and less guttural.

When finally the process had ended, and Jekyll alone now stood by the bureau, Lanyon went across and took his friend's arm. 'Whatever was—?'

Jekyll shook his head. 'Please keep silent about what you have seen,' he said, his voice growing a little stronger.

'You should see someone, get help.' But his friend had already disappeared into the night.

'Return the drawer, dear Lanyon,' Jekyll's disembodied voice called out of the swirling mist.

Some weeks later, Utterson received a visit from Poole, who asked that the lawyer come to the house immediately; his master, it transpired, had locked himself in his laboratory.

'He has been in there for several days now,' Poole breathlessly informed Utterson as the pair strode purposefully through town towards Jekyll's house.

'Moreover,' Poole confided, 'I am becoming increasingly concerned by what I hear from behind the locked door.'

'What sounds do you hear, dear fellow?'

'His voice, sir – it was not my master's voice.'

Sure enough, at Jekyll's house the voice that spoke in response to the butler's insistent

knocking on the laboratory door was considerably
changed – it was hoarse, guttural. 'I do not want
to see anyone,' it said.

'I wonder if the devil has done away with my
master,' Poole whispered.

'You say he's been in there for several days?'

Poole nodded. 'Eight days to be precise, crying
and wailing like a soul demented. And all the
while I have been sent hither and thither, bearing
notes to all the chemists I know – and some
whom I did not know.'

'And what did these notes say?'

'They were for ingredients, sir, for some drug. Every time I brought the stuff back, there would be another note telling me to return it, because it was not pure, and another order to a different firm. He wants this drug very bad, sir, for whatever reason.'

'Do you have one of these notes?'

Frowning, the butler patted his pockets, and produced a crumpled piece of paper which he flattened out before handing to Utterson.

'And was the chemist able to produce what your master requested?' Utterson asked as he read the note.

Poole shook his head with regret. 'Alas, no. I was told that the drug which the doctor wanted was no longer available – apparently he himself had bought the last of it some time previously. So I returned home without it, at which point—' The butler stopped and glanced at the closed door. 'At which point the person in the room – for I can no longer assume that it is my master – grew angry.'

'Well, you should have no concerns, Poole – this is indeed the doctor's hand.'

Poole nodded enthusiastically. 'Yes, Mr Utterson,' he said at last. 'It is the doctor's hand – or, at least, a close facsimile of it – but what matter the hand? I have seen him.'

'Seen him?'

'Yes, sir. It was but for one minute, but the hair stood upon my head like quills. Sir, if that was my master, why had he a mask upon his face? If it was my master, why did he cry out like a rat, and run from me?'

'Was it Mr Hyde?'

'Yes, sir,' Poole confirmed. 'I believe it was.'

Having resolved that the only course of action was to break down the door into Jekyll's laboratory, Utterson dispatched the footman to the other entrance with instructions not to allow anyone ease of passage. Then, armed with axe and poker, they returned to the door.

'Jekyll,' Utterson called loudly. 'I demand to see you.' He paused but there was no reply. 'I give you fair warning. Our suspicions are aroused and I mean to see you. If you do not allow us access then we shall have no alternative but to break down the door.'

'Utterson,' a voice croaked from within, 'for god's sake have mercy.'

'That is not the voice of my friend,' Utterson said softly to the butler. 'It is Hyde's voice. Down with the door, Poole!'

Within minutes, Poole had brought down the heavy door with a succession of bold swings of the axe, and the pair burst into a room that seemed almost tranquil. A fire sputtered in the hearth, drawers were open, their contents visible but neat, and, by the fire, things were laid out for tea while a kettle hummed on the grate.

But in the middle of the floor lay a figure, still twitching.

Utterson bent down to turn over the figure. It was Edward Hyde, but dressed in clothes that were clearly far too big for his frame. 'I fear we are too late,' Utterson said, as he held Hyde's wrist and felt for a pulse. 'It only remains for us to find the body of your master.'

Following an extensive search, Utterson and Poole found no sign of Dr Jekyll, either alive or dead.

'Sir, there's a letter,' Poole exclaimed from the counter, 'and it's addressed to you.'

Utterson went across to the butler and opened the envelope. 'Why, it's Jekyll's will,' said Utterson. 'He has written a new one. And in place of Hyde, your master has placed my own name as beneficiary.' Utterson turned his attention to the counter and discovered a second packet, this one dated and containing two documents – one written by Jekyll himself and one by Dr Lanyon.

'Jekyll must have been here this very day,' Utterson said. 'He cannot have been killed and buried in so short a time. He must have fled, though why should he flee?'

'Perhaps the answer is in those letters,' Poole ventured.

The lawyer nodded. 'Perhaps. But I foresee

that we may yet involve your master in some dire catastrophe.'

Before the night was out, Utterson knew the full extent of his friend's folly. He had read Lanyon's account of Hyde's bizarre transformation earlier in the year. He had read Jekyll's painful disclosure of his determination to increase medical knowledge, without a single concern for his own safety or well-being. And he had read of Henry Jekyll's belief that man was not one entity but two, like the two sides of a coin, one good and one bad. 'If each,' Jekyll had written, 'could be housed in separate identities, life would be relieved of all that was unbearable.'

When he reached the end of the account, Utterson held his head in despair. Alas, his friend had discovered instead that each man must house the whole of himself – both the good and the bad – within one identity and one body. It is the failure to balance these opposing forces within one identity and one body that makes life truly unbearable.

# TAKING THINGS FURTHER

## The real read

This *Real Reads* version of *The Strange Case of Dr Jekyll and Mr Hyde* is a retelling of Robert Louis Stevenson's wonderful and rather frightening short novel. If you would like to read the full novel in all its original splendour, many complete editions are available, from bargain paperbacks to beautifully-bound hardbacks. You should be able to find a copy in your local library or in a charity shop.

## Filling in the spaces

The loss of so many of Stevenson's original words is a sad but necessary part of the shortening process. Although we have omitted little, we have had to make some difficult decisions concerning the sequence of events. The points below will help you to move from this *Real Reads* version of *Dr Jekyll and Mr Hyde* to Robert Louis Stevenson's original.

- Utterson is concerned by the change in his friend's will. His attempt to understand Jekyll's motives begins the process that will eventually reveal the doctor's folly.

- When he meets Hyde for the first time, Utterson considers him deformed and even troglodytic – a troglodyte is a creature that lives below ground and away from the sunlight.

- Utterson believes that Jekyll must have committed some unspeakable crime, the details of which Hyde knows about.

- When confronted, Jekyll explains that his relationship with Hyde is 'one of those affairs that cannot be mended by talking', which suggests that Jekyll recognises very early in the story that he is in danger of losing control.

- In the original, the killing of Sir Danvers Carew is a remarkably brutal passage: 'The old gentleman took a step back, with the air of one very much surprised and a trifle hurt; and at that Mr Hyde broke out of all bounds and clubbed

him to the earth. And next moment, with ape-
like fury, he was trampling his victim under
foot and hailing down a storm of blows, under
which the bones were audibly shattered.'

- When Inspector Newcomen goes with
Utterson to Hyde's rooms they discover many
signs of a double life – 'A closet was filled
with wine; the plate was of silver, the napery
elegant; a good picture hung upon the wall', yet
clothes are strewn around in heaps as though
the place has been ransacked.

- Some time before the close of the story, Dr
Lanyon dies following a short but aggressive
illness. After his friend's death, Utterson
receives a letter from Lanyon marked for his
personal attention, with the additional clause
'in case of his predecease to be destroyed
unread'.

- It is in Henry Jekyll's last letter, in his
own words, that we learn first-hand of all the
horrors he has experienced.

# Back in time

Robert Louis Stevenson wrote *The Strange Case of Dr Jekyll and Mr Hyde* in 1886, at the age of thirty-six. He was already known for the exciting subject matter of his adventure novels and stories of the fantastic, such as *Treasure Island*, a thrilling adventure story of a search for buried gold. The most exciting of his books, however, and certainly the one which achieved greatest immediate acclaim, was his tale of Dr Jekyll and Mr Hyde. Within a few months it sold 40,000 copies, and as the century turned it was estimated to have sold more than 250,000.

Stevenson had long been interested in the idea of the two sides – good and evil – of human character. He lived in a society which greatly valued etiquette, reputation and proper manners. Such civilised behaviour tended to cause people to repress other sides of their characters, such as sensuality, physicality, and anger.

At the same time the British were exploring and conquering new worlds, where society often behaved differently, in a way that Victorians considered 'savage'. Whilst they might fear the 'savage', many Victorians were also fascinated, perhaps because they recognised such tendencies within themselves.

During the nineteenth century, many parts of London had become overcrowded and dirty: poverty and disease were terrible problems. People of Jekyll's class might have chosen to ignore it, but they could not have been unaware of the existence of 'less civilised' people in their midst. Stevenson wanted to explore, in the words of Dr Jekyll, 'man, not as truly one, but truly two'.

Queen Victoria's reign saw great progress in science, technology and medicine. By 1886 anaesthetics and antiseptic were in common use, and people were increasingly interested in the potential of science, which led to considerable experimentation. This gave Stevenson the medical background to his story.

Once Stevenson had found a way to write about the two sides of human nature, he attacked the project with such ferocity that the entire book was probably completed in as little as three days.

# Finding out more

We recommend the following books and websites to gain a greater understanding of Robert Louis Stevenson and the world he lived in.

## Books

- Jenni Calder, *RLS: A Life Study*, Hamilton, 1980.

- Edwin M. Eigner, *Robert Louis Stevenson and Romantic Tradition*, Princeton University Press, 1966.

- Ann Kramer, *Victorians* (Eyewitness Guides), Dorling Kindersley, 1998.

- Terry Deary, *Vile Victorians* (Horrible Histories) Scholastic, 1994.

- Natasha Narayan, *The Timetraveller's Guide to Victorian London*, Timetraveller's Guides, 2004.

## Websites

- http://dinamico.unibg.it/rls/rls.htm
Everything you could possibly want to find out about Robert Louis Stevenson.

- http://www.gradesaver.com/classicnotes/ titles/jekyll/themes.html
A discussion of the similarities between the two states of Jekyll and the two faces of London, one grimy and oppressive and the other welcoming and bustling with excitement.

- http://www.bbc.co.uk/history/british/victorians
The BBC's interactive site about Victorian Britain, with a wide range of information and activities for all ages.

- http://www.gradesaver.com/classicnotes/quiz/ jekyll/1/
See how many questions you get right in this free quiz.

## Films

- *Dr Jekyll and Mr Hyde* (1931) MGM, directed by Rouben Mamoulian.

- *Dr Jekyll and Mr Hyde* (1981) BBC/Second Sight, directed by Alastair Reid.

- *The Dr Jekyll and Mr Hyde Rock and Roll Musical* (2002) Elite, directed by André Champagne.

- *The Strange Case of Dr Jekyll and Mr Hyde* (2006) Image Entertainment, directed by John Carl Buechler.

- *Jekyll* (2007) BBC/Contender. A television version about a fictional modern-day descendent of Jekyll.

## Food for thought

Here are some things to think about if you are reading *The Strange Case of Dr Jekyll and Mr Hyde* or ideas for discussion if you are reading it with friends.

In retelling the story we have tried to recreate, as accurately as possible, Robert Louis Stevenson's original plot and characters. We have also tried to imitate aspects of his style. Remember, however, that this is not the original work; thinking about the points below, therefore, can only help you begin to understand the author's craft. To move forward from here, turn to the full-length version and lose yourself in his exciting tale.

## Starting points

- Give examples from the text of the way the author uses the city itself as a character to create moods.

- Would you say that Utterson is a helpful and well-meaning character, or do you think he comes across as nosy and interfering?

- Why do you think there are no women characters in Stevenson's book? What do you think about the fact that none of the main characters seems to be in an important relationship?

- What do you think are the aspects of Hyde that give most concern to those who encounter him.

## Themes

What do you think Robert Louis Stevenson is saying about the following themes?

- the two sides of human nature

- civilised society and human beings

- scientific experiments

- friendship and honesty

## Style

Can you find paragraphs containing examples of the following?

- the use of exclamation marks

- descriptions of scenery

- the use of short sentences to create suspense

- sentences that use old-fashioned language

Look closely at how these paragraphs are written. What do you notice? Can you write a paragraph in the same style?